A SLAVE OF THE
BIRD MEN

A SLAVE OF THE
BIRD MEN

PAUL V. CWIAKALA

Silk Baron Independent Press
Paterson, New Jersey

To my sister, Kim,
For pushing me to finish my stories and publish.

Table of Contents

Foreword

The Great American Interchange, some assert, was the greatest ecological disaster to strike South America before the advent of humanity. Following the formation of the Isthmus of Panama about 3 million years ago, the relatively isolated South American ecosystem was invaded by North American species. This invasion resulted in direct competition between the unique avian species that dominated the continent and mammalian predators. By and large, the mammals succeeded in nearly every category, resulting in the wholesale extermination of the Phorusrhacids (also known as the "terror birds") and the domination of mammals in the newly formed singular American landmass.

There were exceptions, of course.

One was the large predatory bird Titanis Walleri, which became the only terror bird to successfully migrate north and survived until the arrival of humans about 20,000 years ago. Two others were the Red-Legged and Black-Legged Seriemas of Brazil, Bolivia, and Argentina.

The most famous survivor, however, was the Seriema's larger cousin, Cariama Primitivus - the direct ancestor of Cariama Sapiens, the only other sapient species on Earth besides Homo Sapiens.

Chapter One

20th of January, 1516
Uruguay River, South America

The little boat leapt as it nicked a sandbar near the shore. Nearer still, three of the seven who'd joined the landing party hopped into the rusty yet fresh waters, glad to relieve them of the heat, and guided it to shore. The beach was no more than a yard from the waves to the tree line, and the hazel-colored earth was pristine in both directions. No man had set foot on it before, so Juan Diaz de Solís added his boot print with gusto. A personal friend of His Majesty King Ferdinand, De Solís had taken command of this expedition at his good friend's request.

He had sailed to the New World once before, with Pinzon, but this time he was tasked but a much greater goal: discovering a route to the Pacific and, God willing, onward to India. He kneeled and crossed himself.

All of this had the ship's Cabin Boy shuddering to pieces with excitement. The New World! At just sixteen years old, this pristine wilderness was the furthest Francisco Del Puerto had ever ventured from the uncouth streets of Sanlúcar de Barrameda. Circumstance and some bloodshed had conspired to put him aboard Captain De Solís' caravel, and with some luck after a few years at sea he'd not just be a man - he'd have escaped retribution. Perhaps he'd be a rich free man too, if all the stories of the New World's immense wealth (and the even more immense wealth of the Far East) proved true. Perhaps he wouldn't go back to Spain at all. Perhaps the expedition would conquer itself some small kingdom, and if luck prevailed he'd be an Indian Prince serving the illustrious Emperor Juan the First of China. Francisco wiped sweat from his brow.

Pedro de Alarcón, the voyage's second-in-command, retrieved a flag from the boat and stabbed its shaft into the soil with extra force. Spain's emblem flapped as it caught the breeze. De Solís stood.

"In the name of His Majesty, Ferdinand the Fifth," he said. "I claim this land for Spain and Christendom…"

Whatever further words the Captain had planned to say, Francisco never heard them: De Solís was interrupted by a loud bark. Francisco at first mistook it for a dog's bark, but at that moment an incredible...thing...emerged from the forest: an immense bird. It stood four feet tall, with a short neck and slender black legs, and was covered in mostly gray feathers accented with blues and purples at the tips of its wings and tail. A bushy crest of red feathers erupted from the base of its pointed black beak. Its face reminded Francisco of a magpie.

The creature regarded them for a moment - not the gaze of a dumb beast, but studying the Spaniards as a man would upon stumbling across a half-dozen strangers. It opened its beak and, to Francisco's amazement, unleashed a series of squawks, clicks, and grunts that sounded unlike any birdsong the boy had ever heard. In fact, it sounded less like birdsong and more like...words. Like language.

It was only now, a moment too late, that Francisco truly saw the creature in total: the complicated patterns painted on its beak and legs, the necklaces of bone and feathers hanging from his neck, the satchel it had strapped to its back, its hands - hardly noticeable the way it had them tucked against its chest.

The inch-long sickle claws on each foot's inner toe.

An immense screech and a dozen of the terrible birds sprinted from their hiding places amongst the trees and shrubbery. It couldn't be called a battle - only Captain de Solís' other officer, Francisco Marquina, was able to draw his sword in time, but it did him little good in those final seconds before one bird pounced upon him, its sickle claws digging into his stomach and its sharpened beak puncturing his throat. Pedro de Alarcón only got so far as reaching for his sword before meeting a similar fate. Captain de Solís turned to flee, only to be pushed into the river with a tremendous splash by the bird that leaped onto his shoulders - Francisco heard him scream as two other birds dragged him back onto shore, but didn't watch them tear him to shreds. Francisco and the remaining sailors attempted to jump back into the boat and return to the caravel, but none made it.

Francisco was a mere arm's length away from the boat, yet he too fell to the birds - pushed into the water, his back slashed, his shirt gripped tight as his would-be killer pulled him back to the bloodied shore. Oh God, not now! Not here! Too frightened to think and unable to imagine resistance, Francisco shut his eyes and prayed. He drowned out the screams of those dying around him, of the terrible birds' squawks and screeches, of his wound's pain, and tried desperately to cling to some measure of peace before death. All he could think, however, when he could think was: 'Oh God, oh God, forgive me!' Images of that overcast day back in Sanlúcar de Barrameda repeated themselves in his mind: Poncio's face, the knife, the pool of blood, the blurred alleyways he'd darted through as he fled…

He wasn't sure how long he'd remained that way before he realized he wasn't dead.

Afraid even this slight movement would spell death he looked again and found himself surrounded by corpses. The caravels were in sight, but sailing again - there would be no rescue. The creatures had washed themselves of the blood, however, and one was tending to the beginnings of a…

…a fire.

Francisco wanted to cross himself, but couldn't bring himself to move.

One of the terrible birds at last noticed him and strutted over. It stood over him and, again, regarded him with that strange man-like intelligence. It raised its foot, its sickle claw aimed at Francisco's throat - all the boy could do was shudder and cringe. He fancied himself a man, but dear God he felt little more than a small boy. Not like this…!

Another bird, a head taller and much heavier, appeared and pushed Francisco's would-be killer aside. The shorter bird yelped, the taller bird barked and screeched angrily. He (there could be no doubt it was a 'he' in Francisco's mind) stretched his neck, making him appear even taller and raised his long tail feathers. The smaller bird spread his wings wide, bowed almost as a man would, and backed away. Still standing tall, the taller bird looked over the rest of his companions and belted a long indecipherable string of barks, hisses, and clicks. The rest did not answer, but all seemed to shrink away. When the tall "Leader" bird finished, all the others made a noise and bowed. Francisco was still terrified, but now terrified and confused.

Quietly, in unintelligible voice that could have been hushed words, it said something. As it walked back toward the fire, Francisco came to a horrible realization:

"Oh God, they're not going to kill me."

- - -

Francisco's first day as prisoner of the terrible birds was not one of thoughts, only of emotions and experiences: the tightness of the vines they bound his wrists with, the stinging needles of semi-numbness in his hands and feet, the sound of some poor animal's final scream as it was slain by some unseen monster, the unbearable humidity, the prick of a demon bird's beak in his back if he stumbled or slowed, the wetness of dew as he brushed against tall grass, hunger pangs, the smell of unwashed poultry that wafted off his captors, the sudden end to the forest and emergence onto a great savannah. They made camp on the savannah - the birds feasted on meat and fruit, and then left Francisco the scraps. He avoided the meat, which he believed to be human, but savored the sweet nectar he was able to suck from the fruit scraps.

On the second day, Francisco's senses returned and he attempted to rationalize his situation. He began to study his captors. Their Leader was the biggest and strongest, and his costume the most elaborate. The tattoos on his beak and legs were the most complex, a dazzling array of symbols and colors Francisco could only begin to guess the purpose of. He wore three necklaces of fangs, claws, and feathers, and Francisco noted bracelets and anklets around its wrists and ankles. Robes clasped together at the base of his neck - a front piece wrapped under its belly. Two other segments ran along its backside, met around the tail feathers, were tied together, and then trailed him like two blue streamers. When squawks were exchanged, the Leader would always stand a head taller. The others were costumed more plainly: a single necklace, and simpler patterns on the beak and legs, but similar bracelets and anklets. Seven of the party's thirteen members carried sacks tied to their backsides, or smaller bags that hung from the waist. Two dragged along the bulk of their cargo on primitive animal skin sleds, like pack animals dragging wagons without wheels. From what he could see of the birds' tattoos, they all shared a single symbol: a pair of vertical blue lines at each corner of the mouth.

On the third day, Francisco noticed that some of the barking noises the birds periodically made had a pattern to it: the Leader started, two answered, the Leader repeated, then a different two, and so on until all had done so, then they all barked and squealed together in unison. In a moment of particular clarity, he realized that this wasn't mere noise but a song, and that this constituted the creatures' idea of singing. That night, as he struggled to sleep, Francisco wondered if the devil's children could sing, or if that was only the privilege of the Lord's flock.

On the morning of the fourth day, Francisco awoke before any of the birds. Other than his hands, he wasn't bound - he realized that if he would ever have a chance to escape, it was now. He stood, looked out at the ocean of grass that surrounded him, rising and falling in waves with the breeze, and hesitated. Why not bind his legs when they slept? They had to have foreseen he would try to flee. Unless, of course, flight was useless. The creatures were fast. Perhaps they were so sure of themselves they saw no need to bind him any further. They could catch him again, no matter how far he ran. Even if he did escape, where could he go? Sanlúcar de Barrameda and Spain were an ocean away, and only the Lord knew if any men lived anywhere near here.

He sighed, sat again, and whispered the Lord's Prayer. Francisco had never felt so alone.

It was on the eleventh day that they reached their destination: a town.

Francisco tried to find a better, less flattering, description, but "town" fit far too well. The place was a collection of large nests: enclosed mounds of sticks and branches, each within an area encircled by what amounted to a fence but was really no more than pointed three-foot sticks arranged in rows outlining the borders of...a territory? Property? More birds - some older, some younger, some who he suspected were female based on their sleeker form and lack of crest feathers - looked out "doors" as they passed by. They followed a path, one of many that seemed to snake amongst groups of nest-huts, and moved deeper into what started feel more like an actual city in size. As they passed through other birds in the street, many made shows of respect to the Leader: a series of calls were exchanged, both would display the underside of the wings (which, to Francisco's surprise, seemed to each be uniquely striped in gray, black, violet, blue, and red), and one - never the Leader - would then bow and extend its wings along the ground. This ritual was repeated over and over with surprising quickness but, as they neared what Francisco soon came to believe was the town square, he noted that each bird seemed not to bow as low as the previous, until at last the bow was dropped entirely.

The party's arrival to the square was heralded by a cacophony of barks, and a small crowd of birds formed, the males dressed like the Leader and the females in different but also elaborate costume. They finally stopped in front of a single larger nest-hut decorated with claws, bones, feathers, and other garnishments. The Leader called out and the crowd hushed: all eyes were on the nest-hut. A figure stepped forth: a large male (older than the Leader if Francisco were to guess), his tattoos and costume the most complex yet. The patterns on his legs were a complicated web of symbols that covered every possible inch. He wore robes as the Leader did, but these were white and embroidered with a vine-like pattern and topped by what looked like a poor man's leather saddle - a cape, Francisco guessed. It too had indecipherable patterns stitched into it, and was lined by blue feathers. His bracelets and anklets were made of bone like the others, but had gemstones embedded in them. Most striking, however, was the leather mask worn over his face and upper beak, covered entirely by the same sort of symbols tattooed on the others. At the point where the bird's crest feathers would be, the mask had four long tail feathers, dyed red, stitched into place.

The great bird stepped forward. All of the creatures assembled bowed, their wings and tail feathers stretched and lowered along the ground.

Someone kicked Francisco from behind and he fell face-first into the hard soil of the square. In the moment afterward, he cursed himself for his stupidity: he'd failed to show the Bird King proper reverence.

The King spoke in grand screeches and angry squawks. The Leader responded in short meek whimpers. The Leader spoke, the King cut him off. Their back and forth quickened. The King approached, strutting, his tail raised. The Leader's tail feathers quivered. The King dealt an angry staccato of grunts, screeches, hisses, and caws. The Leader turned his head, exposing his throat. The King ignored the gesture, strutting past the others and toward Francisco. A single powerful kick (cracking a rib), and Francisco was on his back, the King's sickle claw jabbed against his jugular. It looked at him, with eyes that clearly did not see a "him" in front them but an "it". A slight twitch and the King could slice his throat open…

He leaned close to Francisco's face, and hissed slow enough for him to make out specific words:

"*Vull faun kad ry us thus tao thu ut guv gu, wo thut da kolloeni gus,*" the King said. "*Tosorduo do, woliothaar!*"

Slowly, carefully, the King cut a shallow scratch across Francisco's throat, enough to hurt but not fatal. He kicked the boy again and then left him, cackling more of his unintelligible bird-speak as he strutted back to the giant nest-hut. The Leader said something, the King didn't respond. As everyone at last relaxed and stood again, Francisco glanced toward the Leader and knew that the blasted beast had saved his life for the second time.

Chapter Two

Francisco was a slave.

This fact didn't occur to him until several days into his new life amongst the birds. In retrospect it was obvious: he was a prisoner, captured in battle and spared for reasons he'd yet to discern. Had these been men he'd have assumed it outright, but being that these were beasts his instincts were that they intended to eat him. It was only after the King had spared his life that he realized this was not the case.

Following the audience with the King, Francisco was brought to the Leader's house a short distance from the town's square and was forced to attempt to sleep in a hollowed out tree in the corner of the property. He watched the sky turn from blue to pink to black, and the waxing Moon rise. As the air cooled, he hugged his legs for warmth.

This was his punishment, wasn't it? He killed a man and fled halfway around the world to escape justice, so God set these beasts on him. He thought of Poncio again. He'd never had any love for the boy; the two had always been rivals of one sort or another. They had fought before, sure, but this time there had been an extra ferocity to the bout. Francisco didn't remember drawing the knife. He remembered the look on Poncio's face, though, as clear as if he were sitting beside him now: the sudden paleness, the widened eyes, the pained little gasp as Francisco pulled back the blade.

The blood. Oh God, there was so much blood.

What should he have done? Should he have waited and watched Poncio die? Was his crime the dishonor of killing and the cowardice of running away? Or was it as simple as breaking that most succinct of God's commandments? Either way, the deed was done. He fled to the harbor, talked his way onto the crew of the first ship he could find, and abandoned what little life he had in Sanlúcar de Barrameda.

Now? Maybe he should have stayed and faced judgment after all.

"KREE!"

The screech startled Francisco awake before he'd realized he'd fallen asleep. Standing a few paces away was a bird he'd never seen before. He was much older than the Leader and his whole body dyed in a complicated pattern of swirling colorful stripes. He wore nothing. He gestured with his right hand, touching his chest three times then and drew a circle in midair.

"*Kue thus* Otak," he said. When Francisco didn't react, he sighed and then displayed the undersides of his wings as the others had done when greeting each other.

"Otak," he said. Was this his name?

"Otak," Francisco repeated, and then pointed at himself. "Francisco."

The old bird seemed somewhere between annoyed and disinterested in the reply.

"*Kue gus roi woliothaar*," Otak said. Francisco hadn't a clue what he meant - he could just barely make out individual words from the screeches. Satisfied that Francisco was awake, the old bird presented a small wooden slab of food (a sweet mush) and water. Francisco noted that this was not just a piece of bark torn from a tree, but had been worked: sawed into a roughly rectangular shape, and each long end had a pair of notches on the top and bottom (to make holding with the beak easier, no doubt).

When Francisco had finished, he offered the slab back.

"Thank you," he said.

Otak slapped it away with his wing and assumed the same assertive posture he had seen the Leader and the King display.

"*Thu eki gus, woliothaar*," he said. "*Tovau!*"

Francisco stared. What did he want from him? The old bird started to growl.

"*Tovau kad* Otak!"

Was he demanding submission? Respect? Francisco thought back and recalled that others had bowed when the Leader and the King had postured this way, so he lowered his head. Otak snorted, but seemed satisfied by the gesture.

Otak herded Francisco to the Leader's nest-hut: it was not much larger than most he had seen so far, but the land that surrounded it was twice the size of his neighbors' properties. From a distance it looked little more than a large pile of sticks, but there seemed to be a method to the chaos and from his fleeting glance through the door it seemed divided into rooms inside like a person's home.

Otak made him stand outside until three birds emerged: the Leader, and two females. These hens were about the same height as the Leader, but a slimmer sort of creature: their beaks more slender, their heads more narrow, their chests more petite but legs and posterior of similar, if not larger, size than a male's. They lacked the crest feathers on the head and their tail feathers were far smaller, though they still retained the inch-long sickle claws on each foot. Both wore green robes, though theirs were worn differently than the Leader's: wrapped around the base of the neck and then crossed across their chests. A second piece, a cape or cloak, covered their backs. They each wore beaded necklaces that crisscrossed up their necks and rested at last on the bridge of their beaks, though he could not see what held them in place. They wore bone bands on each thigh, while their beaks and legs were tattooed as the Leader's - although, in this case, Francisco noticed that the younger of the two females had fewer tattoos than the elder.

Otak made him bow, spreading his arms out as the birds would do, and hold that position. The Leader chatted with the females for a few moments, until at last the older female barked, stretched her neck and raised her tiny tail feathers. The Leader silenced and bowed slightly, while the younger female bowed fully. The older female strutted a slow circle around Francisco, pecking and poking him as one might when inspecting an animal one sought to buy. He supposed she must have been satisfied, because when finished she purred - the exact sound a content cat would make - and, in a very cat-like manner, lovingly rubbed her face against the Leader's.

They shared a few more words - Francisco was just

beginning to make out individual syllables from the inhuman noises with some regularity - before another bird he did not know arrived, displayed his wings, bowed and at last spoke up. He repeated a single sound (Word? Phrase?) twice in the short exchange that followed between him and the Leader: "*oka-CLICK-ee tee*". The Leader and the hens exchanged bows, and then the cocks left them.

The Leader was not yet out of sight when the elder hen pressed Francisco into servitude. She led Francisco and Otak to another end of the property and an old lean-to. She said something to the old bird and gestured with her head toward Francisco. By his reaction, Francisco guessed Otak wasn't pleased but nevertheless bowed and obeyed: he retrieved what looked to be a fishing net from the lean-to with his beak and dropped it at the boy's feet. Francisco looked from the net, to Otak, to the Hen.

"I don't understand," he said. "What do you want me to do? Do you want me to fish? I don't know much about fishing with a pole, let alone fishing with a net."

The Hen was indifferent. She turned back toward the nest hut, while Otak began to growl and assume the dominant stance again.

"Yes, yes, fine! As you command, my Lord," Francisco said, bowing and kneeling. Otak snorted again and set about pulling at the edges of the net with his beak, stretching it out to its full size. Then, he sat (to Francisco's eyes, exactly as a rooster would) and then spoke. When it became clear Francisco didn't understand, he gestured for Francisco to sit. With his little clawed hands he picked up part of the net and pointed at it.

"The net?"

Otak hissed, but it was neither angry nor aggressive. It sounded like he had said "set", and he had accompanied it with a little gesture: a forward motion with his head and neck.

He pointed again. Francisco looked more closely: the old bird was pointing at a broken strand. Carefully and quickly, he tied the two errant pieces back together.

Francisco nodded. Looking over the net, it was quite a mess: much of it looked damaged. He picked one part, tied it together, and pointed.

"Thiss," Otak said, with a rightward twitch of the head. Did that mean 'yes'? If so, that meant 'set' was 'no'. As they worked, Francisco picked up a little more of his captors' language: "Good" was "it", "bad" was "you-awn", "correct" was "CLICK-it", "incorrect" was "nee". When they finished with the net, the Hen returned with their next task: carving hooks out of unidentifiable yellowed brown bones. After that, they were tasked with "tidying" the Leader's land: the birds seemed to prefer bare upturned soil around their nest huts and the rest of the day was spent just pulling up every little weed sproutling. At sundown, Otak led him back to the hollowed out tree, where more sweet mush and a saucer of water waited for him. After another uncomfortable night, it all began again at dawn: the sweet mush, Otak asserting his dominance, the chores, then dinner (this time with a few morsels of meat) and sleep yet again. None of the tasks assigned were difficult, though he was afforded little time to rest. After the first few days he was left to his own devices while working, although usually Otak or another servant was nearby keeping watch.

The Leader would come and go, though rarely would he give any attention to Francisco's presence. He was someone important amongst the birds, a Nobleman perhaps, as evidenced by the bows he received from visitors. At home, though, the Lady ruled, and here she was the Master. While the Leader rarely bowed to others, he always bowed to the Lady. Whereas he always stood tall and strutted in the presence of other males, he was always submissive to her. When not submissive, he treated her as an equal. Francisco puzzled over the nature of the second hen: she always deferred to the Lady, and did not seem to have the same standing with the Leader. She must be the less favored of the Leader's wives.

Whereas the Lady spent most her day giving orders to Francisco or the servants, the younger wife attended to two adolescent birds, both female and both dressed similar to the Leader's wives but without the capes or necklaces. They spent most of their day sunning or singing, their voices clearly more suited to music than the males who captured him, while the younger wife brought them food, preened them, and doted over them as a good mother hen should. When the Leader returned at night to sleep, they joined him and the wives inside the nest-hut. At night, a hole in the roof would let out a light stream of smoke. Francisco was never allowed inside, not that he could imagine fitting well in such a small space anyway.

While eating his dinner one evening, Francisco noticed that one of the servants lived in the nest hut next door. Over the following days he realized most of the Leader's visitors and the Lady's servants lived in the same group of nest-huts (Ward?) as they did.

All that is, except for Otak.

Otak lived in a much smaller nest hut on the opposite side of the Leader's property from Francisco, a shack in comparison to the family's home.

"He's a slave too," Francisco said to no one.

It made sense. He was often assigned most of the same chores as Francisco, and seemed just as subservient to the Lady. Perhaps that was why he seemed so adamant about asserting his higher status? He was no longer the lowest rung in this family's ladder.   Francisco fell asleep wondering how Otak had ended up in this predicament.

Watching so many comings and goings, Francisco was able to work out the meanings of the calls: "thu-kom-gu", "thu-kom-lo", and "thu-rye-gu" all seemed to more or less mean "I greet you". The sounds that followed were, he assumed, a name - but, what someone would be called in that last phrase would change. For instance, the Leader would call the Lady "It-wu-ah", but the younger wife called her "Deo-na" and the servants would call her "Deo-ti Ere-ter-is". It was just as difficult to work out the Leader's name: his wives would call him "Rawd-hue-ah", but all else either "Oka-CLICK-ee tee" or "Ere-ter".

One morning when the Lady came to dole out the day's instructions, Francisco decided to test what he had learned.

"Thu-kom-gu…ah…Deo-ti…Ere-ter-is," he said, with a bow. Otak seemed stunned. The Lady stood tall and raised her tail feathers.

"Yes," the Lady said, in her tongue. "You will both come with me now. There is work to do."

Chapter Three

"Get up!"

The Leader kicked the tree again - it shook, little bits of dirt and dust rained on Francisco's head.

"Up, up!" he said. "It's already daylight. How can you sleep so late? Up, you lazy *theth*!"

Francisco scrambled out of his hole and bowed.

"Yes, master! Sorry master!"

The Leader snorted. He bent his head and scratched an itch under his beak with a sickle claw.

"Enough groveling," he said. Francisco looked up and was surprised: the Leader wasn't wearing his usual costume. In fact, he wasn't wearing anything at all! Had he not recognized the bird's voice, he may not have recognized him. "You will accompany me, human."

"Yes, master."

The Leader did not lead him to the nest hut, as usual, but instead to the road and the little square just in front of his land. There they met a crowd of birds, all of them as naked as the Leader: their beaks and legs were still tattooed, of course, but beyond that, and the identifying marks of the wings' undersides, he couldn't tell one bird from the other.

Except for Otak, of course. The colorful swirling patterns dyed onto his feathers made him stand out of any crowd. He did not seem pleased to see Francisco, though that was normal.

Everyone revealed the undersides of their wings and bowed, some more deeply than others, at the Leader's arrival. He turned to one of the birds closest.

"Have all gathered?" he said.

"Yes." It was the Lady, Francisco knew that voice anywhere. "We now have everyone."

"Then, let's depart."

They navigated the narrow streets toward the large square and the King's royal nest hut. Francisco, still groggy, fell in line beside Otak. He leaned over and mustered the little bit of language he'd picked up:

"I greet you, friend Otak."

Otak glanced his way, but did not answer.

"What happen?" Francisco said. "Where go we?"

Behind them, one of the birds hissed and pecked Francisco's backside. Fine, fine, no talking! He rubbed the spot where the beak struck.

Up until today, his days had begun to bleed together as he settled into the routine of servitude. The days had cooled since his arrival (perhaps it had been unseasonably warm?) and settled into a more comfortable warmth. The more he had observed the Leader's family and learned of their language, the more curious he had become of the

town surrounding them.   How many birds lived here?
What lay beyond the town? Were there other towns, other
kingdoms? How far did their King's domain stretch? He
knew that there were Men in the New World, where were
they?   Francisco had many questions, and no way to
answer them without leaving the Leader's land.   Until
today he'd never been given an opportunity to do so.

The Leader stopped his flock at the square's entrance.
The square itself was empty, but Francisco saw other
crowds gathered and gathering at the other entrances. All
waited, more or less silent beyond the chattering of chicks
and the hushes of their mothers. At last, three birds
emerged from the King's hut: an elderly female in bloody-
red robes that trailed behind her, an animal skin ruff at the
base of the head, and a headdress that draped two trios of
blue feathers down the sides of her face. She was followed
by two, much younger, females dressed as the Lady usually
did, carrying the ends of her robe in their beaks. The three
stopped just beyond the King's land. The elder Hen looked
to each of the groups and squeaked:

"Good *Kio Koklinenis. Duahib* purrs in delight that
the six clans of the *Auldtheu* have come together in peace
to honor her." She turned to the group closest to her.
"*Laaptui-ti*, what gifts do you have for our *Paku*?"

A large bird, his face and beak sporting large long
scars that snaked from his left eye to halfway down his
neck, stepped forward.

"Honored *Naeyvolis*..." Francisco recognized that
voice. Who was he? "...the Laaptui present these gifts."

A dozen or so birds entered the square and left a
feast's worth of food - deer, pig-like creatures, fish, nuts
and fruits and vegetables Francisco didn't recognize - at
the Naeyvolis' feet, each bird bowing deeply to her as they
did so.   Several birds, a couple looking somewhat

malnourished, were forced out into the square and made to sit along with the food.

"Duahib accepts your gifts," she said and turned to the Leader's group. "Oka'ee-ti, what gifts do you have for our Paku?"

"Honored Naeyvolis," the Leader said. "The Oka'ee presents these gifts."

A train of birds from the Leader's group did as the Laaptui had done and carried a feast's worth of food into the square. When they finished, Otak pushed Francisco forward.

"Go."

He stepped into the square, followed close behind by Otak and other dozen or so slaves owned by the Leader's clan. The mumblings amongst the assembled birds rose. Francisco sensed that all eyes were on him, though none more piercing than the Naeyvolis: her pale green eyes were fixed, her body may as well have been carved of stone. A bead of sweat dripped of Francisco's nose. Was he supposed to do something? He hadn't paid close enough attention when the Laaptui slaves had been herded into the square. Was he supposed to bow? They were more than halfway to her now. Why had they pushed him to the front of the line?! The Leader spoke to her as if she were his superior. But, he didn't bow when she appeared! What was he supposed to –

They were a yard from the Naeyvolis when he hesitated. He opened his mouth to speak, but remembering that the first batch of slaves had said nothing closed it again. He bit his lip, and then, slowly, bowed in the manner the birds had taught him.

The square turned silent.

When Francisco rose again, Otak and the other slaves were staring at him: most wide-eyed and beaks agape, a few appearing rather angry. The Naeyvolis had not reacted at all. Was that a mistake? Unsure what to do, he sat near the other slaves - albeit, a good few paces separate from them. The mumblings rose again, then subsided. She looked down at him, neither speaking nor gesturing. At last, she looked to the Leader.

"Duahib accepts your gifts."

The Naeyvolis moved on to the next group and the ritual repeated, again and again, until all six clans had presented their gifts.

"You have done well this *Koklineni*, and Duahib sighs in contentment," the Naeyvolis said. "You honor her with your gifts, now you may honor her with your actions. Eat! Drink! Today we enjoy life at its height and to its fullest, because that is what our Paku commands."

The crowd roared "Kio Koklinenis!" and flooded the square. Before long, the clans had intermingled and the square teemed with activity. Some birds sat beside fires, pecking at roasting meats. Chicks chased each other to-and-fro, adults danced: a process of fancy footwork while raising a wing above the head and moving in a slow circle, or in a figure eight pattern if with a partner. Still others milled about, chatting. A small army of birds carried in an enormous animal-skin bowl and filled it with some yellow-brown liquid, into which any and every bird nearby would dip its beak for a drink. Drumbeats and rattles nearly drowned out speech. Francisco's nose was overwhelmed by smoke and by the aromas of roast venison and other meats he couldn't identify.

"It's a holiday", Francisco said to no one, bewildered. That the birds would celebrate holidays as men did had not occurred to him. True, he had already suspected the birds had religion (nothing directly over heard, just an intuition), so it made sense that they would celebrate feast days and holy days.

After a couple of hours, Francisco grew bored with watching the festival. He inched his way back toward the other slaves, most of whom sat in a group surrounding the small mountain of food.

"I greet you," he said to the nearest one. The bird, who hadn't noticed Francisco's approach, yelped in surprise and cringed.

"Sorry!   Sorry!" Francisco said, then shifted to Spanish: "I didn't mean to frighten you." He switched back to the birds' language again: "We talk, yes?"

The bird, and the couple others he'd been talking to before the interruption, only responded with widened eyes. One trembled.   The exchange caught all the slaves' attention: those that didn't seem frightened or disturbed looked angry. Several, including Otak, stood.

Francisco sighed, raised his hands, and inched away again.

"I sorry," he said. The slaves settled again and went back to ignoring him.

At last, they brought food and drink to the slaves. One bird wandered over to him and dropped a whole roast leg of what could be pork.

"I greet you!" the bird said. His words were slurred. "Good Kio Koklinenis!"

"All this?" Francisco said. "All for me?"

The drunken cock gestured 'yes'. Francisco took a big bite out of the meat and chewed slowly, savoring every bite. It tasted like pork, but there was a hint of fishiness to the flavor that convinced him it had to be something else. Whatever it was, after weeks of mush and months more of gruel at sea it was the most delicious thing he'd ever tasted. His drunken benefactor left him for a few minutes and returned with a drink. Francisco took a sip and couldn't believe his tongue.

"This is alcohol!"

It tasted like sweet swill, but there was no mistaking it. He downed the rest in two gulps.

"Sot," Francisco thanked him. "*Gio gu?*" When the bird didn't respond, he repeated in Spanish: "Who are you? What is your name? I am Francisco. Fran-cis-co. You?"

"Ran-sis-ko?"

The bird took a moment to puzzle out what he meant.

"I am Oka'ee Kothidy Eyeu," he said, displaying the undersides of his wings. "You may call me Kothidy."

"Thank you, Kothidy," Francisco said. "Are you related to my master? *Gu dill aud ti?*"

"Yes. Oka'ee-ti Ereter is my cousin," Kothidy said - Francisco was getting better at understanding the birds' speech. This was the closest he'd had to a normal conversation since he was captured.

"What is...?" Francisco waved his hand around, indicating the festival around them. Kothidy tilted his head.

"Kio Koklinenis?" he asked.

"Yes."

Kothidy recognized the confusion on Francisco's face, much to the Spaniard's surprise.

"Kio. 'Kio' is..." He stomped his foot. "We are in the usqu." Usqu...square? He then gestured toward the square's borders. "The usqu kio over there."

"Oh, 'end'! I understand."

"Koklineni..." Kothidy tilted his head and squinted an eye as he thought of an answer. "Koklineni is now, the time of warmth and dryness."

"*Verano*," Francisco said. "My word is '*verano*'."

Kothidy attempted to pronounce the word, but the closest he could manage was 'derano'.

"So, Kio Koklinenis," Francisco said. "The Summer's End."

"Yes," Kothidy said. "Does your kind not honor the close of summer and Duahib's month?"

"We do," Francisco said and left it at that. The festivities reminded him a little of the Feast of Saint Martin…if the feast were a pagan festival. Something across the square caught Kothidy's attention.

"Oh…there is Tok. She's so much fun! We should talk to her." He stumbled a few steps into the crowd, then turned back. "Come with me."

Francisco blinked.

"No, no, I sit, I eat" he said. Kothidy erupted in a staccato of "CRAW CRAW CRAW"s. Was he…laughing? He gestured with his head and left wing. "You're funny! Tok will love you. Come!"

This was a bad idea.

No sooner had Francisco stood and taken a few steps did Kothidy vanish into the crowd, just another bird he couldn't tell apart from the rest.

Someone shouted alarm. The birds around him halted whatever they were doing and turned toward Francisco. He paled.

Really bad idea.

He offered an awkward smile and took a step back.

"I see you've made it out of your tree, *woliothaar*."

Francisco, startled by the voice so close behind him, spun, tripped over himself, and fell on his ass. The large bird standing over him was the Laaptui-ti, he recognized the scars.

…No. Wait. That voice. He knew that voice. Idiot! As naked as the rest, Francisco hadn't recognized the Bird King again. He scrambled to kowtow at the King's feet.

"Y-yes, my…um…" Oh God, he'd never picked up

the word for King! *"Uh...sí, mi Rey! Perdona mi insolencia!"*

The King growled.

"Did you think we wouldn't notice a *meu aud Restat* wandering about?" he said. "Do you think we are fools?"

"N-no!"

The Square had turned silent.

"Did someone tell you to leave the gifts?" the King said. Francisco pretended not to understand. The King narrowed his eyes.

"Leave him be, father."

Another bird, not quite as large as the King, stepped up from behind. Francisco was too frightened to notice any family resemblance.

"Yes, stop spoiling the mood, Sukoktheu," a female said. "Look, you've interrupted everyone."

After a moment, the King relented.

"You're right, of course," he said. The King turned away. "Ereter, in the future please keep your *ithnaar* on a shorter leash. It would be unfortunate for both you and this creature if I lost my temper."

The Leader - he'd been standing an arm's reach away from the King and Francisco hadn't recognized him! - stepped forward.

"As you command, *Atiti.*"

The Square returned to its festivities while the Leader (no, "Ereter") snatched Francisco's tattered collar in his beak and half dragged, half guided him back to the other slaves.

"I sorry," Francisco said. "I do wrong?"

Ereter stood over him in the dominant stance.

"*Ithnaareni* cannot leave the gifts," he said. It wasn't difficult to deduce that an 'ithnaar' was a 'slave'. "Sukoktheu already disapproves of your presence in

Atilatius. Do not give him an excuse to kill you."

Odd, Ereter didn't sound angry.

"Yes, master," Francisco said. Ereter lowered his head and spoke quietly.

"You did well today, honoring the Naeyvolis," he said. "I knew sparing you was the right decision. You have impressed many, and I suppose me most importantly. It perturbed our Atiti too, which is a nice addition."

"Thank you," Francisco said.

"You speak well enough too, considering it wasn't so long ago that you could speak nothing," Ereter said. "You're young and strong, so I'd planned for you serve my wife as Otak has done. But, after tonight…I think I may have a better use for you."

"Yes, Master."

Ereter stood tall again.

"Wait here and do not move," he said. "We will fetch you."

Ereter vanished into the crowd once more.

Francisco sat and spent the rest of his day watching the festivities. Some of the birds watched back, muttering amongst themselves about the presence of "the Oka'ee-ti's woliothaar". A few seemed genuinely curious, although none had the courage to approach. He overheard more than one ask, "Is he a good one? Is he not a servant of Restat?"

Francisco hadn't a clue who or what Restat could be.

The chicks made a game of seeing how close they could sneak up on him before he noticed, and he amused himself by playing along. Eventually, they grew bored and moved on to something else. The sun set, and the celebrations grew more rowdy as the birds grew ever more intoxicated.

One dropped a hand-sized slab of meat, venison by

the smell, at Francisco's feet.

"You look hungry again," Kothidy said. "Eat."

"Thank you." Francisco tore into it with gusto.

"Why didn't you tell the Atiti that I was responsible? That I told you to leave the others?"

"You kind to me," Francisco said in between mouthfuls. "I no want you trouble."

Kothidy looked into the crowd, and seemed to watch the flames in one of the fire pits.

"You didn't have to do that."

Chapter Four

Months passed.

In the weeks following Summer's End, the weather had cooled and the rain had picked up. While sleeping in a tree's trunk may have been somewhat acceptable during the dry season, it was a sure recipe for pneumonia now that the rains had returned. So, with the little free time afforded to him each day, he had slowly constructed a little shelter in the shade of his tree: a circle of timbers about his height in diameter, stabbed into the ground much like the birds' perimeter fences and bound together with some twine he'd been given. He filled in the gaps with mud, grass, and leaves, then topped it off more branches and larger leaves. Between the tree and his meager roof, he hoped it would be enough to keep most of the rain out.

A royal villa it was not, but it would do. He'd lived in

worse.

Following Summer's End, Lord Ereter had taken Francisco under his wing (figuratively, that is) and Francisco joined him as he went about his day-to-day business, serving as a personal attendant. Ereter instructed Francisco to observe everything: the manner of speaking, how the birds carried themselves, and how those 'with rank' behaved towards others either higher or lower than themselves.

The birds organized their society as any other bird would: with a pecking order. The strong lorded over the weak in a neat and easy sequence from King Sukoktheu all the way down to the lowliest peasant's slave.

Atilatius was divided into four castes, each caste consisting of its own smaller pecking order - even if the strongest of one caste was stronger than the weakest of a higher caste, the higher caste-member was considered higher in the pecking order by virtue of blood. At the top of society stood the Auldtheu, a ruling class made up of hunters, warriors, and traders. Being the strongest of the birds, they naturally held the highest positions in society and the Atilatian throne. He knew there were six Auldtheu clans, and their wards were gathered together around the large square - Francisco had come to call it "King's Square" to differentiate it from all the others. He did not know much of the politics amongst the Auldtheu beyond Lord Ereter's distaste for the King, and that the Laaptui clan had ruled Atilatius for five generations.

Next were the Degioeki, the laborers and workers of Atilatius. There were eight Degioeki clans, and their wards resided to the north and west, along the river. Although nearly as strong as the Auldtheu, the Degioeki were not as skilled in the art of killing and combat. Below them were the five clans of the Vulthaar, the city's craftsmen and weavers - skilled with tools and the finer uses of the sickle claw, but very much lacking in brute physical strength.

At the bottom were the Ithnaareni, slaves like himself. The slaves too had a pecking order, but their ranks were determined by the positions of their masters. By this logic, since Lord Ereter seemed to be amongst the highest ranked of the Auldtheu, Francisco as his slave was amongst the highest ranked Ithnaareni. It also afforded him some leeway in his dealings with the birds, since an insult or slight against Francisco could be interpreted as such against Lord Ereter. That could be useful someday.

Simple following and observing soon graduated to simple tasks Ereter was confident enough (and, to Francisco's surprise, apparently trustworthy enough) to entrust with him, usually to serve as a messenger boy or courier between Lord Ereter and one of his associates. Beyond bowing to the Naeyvolis, Francisco wasn't sure what brought on his owner's sudden trust in him to do this much. It felt unwarranted.

Otak hated it, though, so Francisco accepted this trust and this duty eagerly.

Some days were still the same as before, and on those days Otak made a point to be a bully. It made the days he wasn't off doing his owner's bidding all the more unbearable.

As the weather cooled, Lord Ereter was kind enough to provide him with a fur blanket. It wasn't particularly warm, but it was better than nothing. Francisco took to wearing the blanket like a cloak. If the chitterings amongst Ereter's wives and daughters meant anything, the birds thought it made him look ridiculous.

- - -

"Oka'ee-ti!"

Francisco looked up from pulling weeds: Kothidy was barreling up the footpath from the road. Ereter shouted something unintelligible from inside the house - Kothidy stopped as if he'd walked into a tree. He tried to stand very still as he waited for his Lord to emerge, but only managed to be twitchy.

"Thukomgu," Francisco said. Kothidy yelped, but calmed slightly when he saw who had spoken.

"Thukomgu, Ransisko," he said.

"Is all well?"

"Yes." He scratched at the ground. "No...no. I..."

Before he could make sense, Ereter stepped outside.

"Ah, thukomgu, my cousin," he said, and displayed his wings' undersides. Kothidy fell to the ground immediately, his tail feathers and wings stretched along the ground. It was the most exaggerated bow Francisco had ever seen from any of the birds.

"Thuryegu, wise and honorable Oka'ee-ti!" Kothidy said. Ereter tilted his head, as puzzled as Francisco.

"...Kothidy, what are you doing?"

"Oka'ee-ti!" Kothidy was shouting and barking his words in an unusual way. "I humbly implore you to grant me permission to marry your second daughter!"

Ereter's head jerked back and eyes widened.

"Tokovudea?"

"Yes, my Leader!" Kothidy said. "I have been granted a property by my father and have built a house. I am strong, and I am capable!"

Ereter snorted.

"Stand up."

"Yes, Oka'ee-ti," Kothidy said, his bravado clearly spent.

"How many years are you?" Ereter said.

"Eight and seven, this season."

"And what is your place in the Order?"

"…Iopift-Gei Veo Re." Kothidy sounded depressed. Francisco wasn't surprised - if he understood Atilatian numbering and ranking right, 1,037 was a low place amongst the Auldtheu.

"You have reached the marriage age and yet you are low in the Order," Ereter said. "It would be thoughtless and irresponsible of me if I agreed to your request."

"But, Oka'ee-ti…!"

Ereter raised his tail feathers, Kothidy cut himself off and bowed his head.

"I have already promised Tokovudea to Oka'ee Ithtee and Tulluedea to Vigsi Elmacade," Ereter said. His voice softened. "There are plenty to choose from, Kothidy. Why my second daughter?"

"…I love her," Kothidy said. "I have for some time."

"I see, you've succumbed to So's will," Ereter said. "You have my pity, but you are too late." He turned away. "Go home."

Ereter went back inside. Kothidy remained, silent, for a few moments. He whispered something, too quietly for Francisco to hear, before leaving.

Otak, annoyed as usual, pecked Francisco's back.

"Stop stalling, second slave!" he said.

Francisco sighed and returned to his work.

- - -

Francisco was returning from another simple errand when he ran into Lord Ereter in the street.

"Ah, good, there you are," Ereter said. He spoke quickly, his wings and tail feathers fidgeted. "You will come with me. Now."

Ereter didn't wait for his slave to respond before rushing off. Francisco scrambled after him.

"What is wrong, Master?" Francisco struggled to keep pace. His grasp of the language had improved rather dramatically over the course of just a few months. "Has something happened?"

"Laaptui Urtu has issued a challenge to Sukoktheu," Ereter said.

"The first son of the Atiti?"

"Yes," Ereter said. "There hasn't been a challenge to the Order in fifteen years, not since Sukoktheu defeated Laaptui Oqyeys and claimed Atiti. If Sukoktheu falls, a new Order must be determined."

"The entire Order?" Francisco said. He took Ereter's silence to mean 'yes', and shuddered at the prospect. By his amateur count, there were as many as 20,000 cocks, hens, and chicks in Atilatius. A reshuffling of the social order, if anything like the reshuffling in barnyard flocks, would be rather bloody.

A crowd had already gathered by the time they reached King's Square. Ereter forced his way to the front, Francisco hugged close to his wake. In front of the King's hut paced Laaptui Urtu, Francisco recognized him as the young male who'd intervened on his behalf months earlier on Summer's End. He was lean, but seemed strong: heavy legs, a muscled neck, sharp-looking sickle claws and beak-tip. His tattoos still seemed fresh. He wore little more than his bracelets and anklets - his clothing and necklaces lay on the ground, torn off. Back and forth, back and forth. In a short line, his eyes never off his father's house.

Between Urtu and the hut stood a few hens, their caws and hisses sounded desperate. The way they bowed and flapped their wings seemed fearful. Francisco couldn't make out all of it, but what he could sounded like pleas for

Urtu to rescind his challenge. Their pleas went ignored.

A male, Francisco recognized him as an Oka'ee, displayed his wings and bowed to Ereter. He couldn't recall his name.

Ereter returned the display.

"Explain."

"Laaptui Urtu and the Atiti were speaking of many matters in the Atiti's house, as you know they often do," he replied. "I am told that the topic of conversation moved of its own will to you, my Leader, and your ithnaar."

"The woliothaar?" Ereter said.

"Yes. The Atiti expressed his disapproval…"

"I am well aware of the Atiti's thoughts on this matter," Ereter said.

"Yes, of course, Oka'ee-ti. Laaptui Urtu spoke favorably of you and of your plans for the woliothaar. The Atiti was not pleased. Harsh words were spoken, and Urtu left in a hurry."

"I don't understand," Ereter said. "How did it come to…"

"I am getting to it, my Leader," the cock said. "Later, not long ago, Laaptui Urtu returned to the square incensed, raving. He and the Atiti argued again, in part about your ithnaar, and in part over some matter known only by the two of them. Urtu let Restat's will get the better of him, and in his anger issued the challenge."

"And the Atiti accepted?" Ereter stamped his feet and huffed. "Sukoktheu, you addled, arrogant, prideful…"

King Sukoktheu stepped out of his hut. The square hushed, and bowed. He raised his tail feathers and craned his neck - he wore only his anklets, bracelets, and mask-crown.

"It seems we've drawn an audience, Orthieu." Sukoktheu paused, raised his right wing and nibbled at an itch underneath. "Beasts hungry for the scraps."

He glanced at his son: Urtu, alone, had not bowed.

"Arrogance is unbecoming," Sukoktheu said.

"Says the arrogant and the thoughtless," Urtu replied. The King's eyes narrowed. He loosened the mask-crown with a finger's talon and let it fall off. He stepped forward. The small crowd separating father and son dispersed, Francisco and the rest broke their obeisance. Everyone granted them a wide berth.

Sukoktheu and Urtu circled each other, their sickle claws twitching with each step. Urtu hissed. Sukoktheu shook his head and raised his tail feathers. Urtu gestured 'No,' and raised his own tail. Sukoktheu didn't take the gesture well: he leaped at Urtu, wings propelling him forward, and lashed out with his sickle claws. Urtu leaped aside, and then dodged as his father kicked again. Pressing his advantage, the King rushed at Urtu and the pair pecked at each other with their beaks: Sukoktheu missed, but Urtu struck the King's right shoulder. Sukoktheu recoiled, fresh blood stained his feathers. Urtu raised his tail again. Sukoktheu responded by stretching and flapping his wings.

"Must you ask?" he said. Urtu huffed, and the two began circling each other again. They traded several feints, prodding each other for weaknesses. As if responding to an unheard signal, the two suddenly leaped at each other and traded kicks. Urtu screeched, a bloody gash emerged across his stomach. Rage overtaking reason, Urtu charged at his father. The two toppled, Urtu's beak clamped onto Sukoktheu's and the pair grappled, wings and claws and legs kicking and flailing. With a great heave, Sukoktheu broke free and stumbled away, bloodied and bruised. Urtu stood - just as bloodied, but tall and defiant. He raised his tail feathers. The King tripped and fell.

"Concede!" Urtu said.

"No."

"Very well!"

Urtu leaped at Sukoktheu again. The King rolled over and lashed out with both his sickle claws. Urtu barked surprise as he flew helplessly into Sukoktheu's kicks. Sukoktheu twisted his legs and a small geyser of blood erupted from Urtu's slashed throat. He tossed his son aside. Sukoktheu stood, suddenly seeming much stronger than he had only moments earlier.

"Do you concede?" he said.

Urtu tried to stand, but could do no better than two steps and a bloody gurgle. He collapsed. Sukoktheu turned to the crowd of spectators, and raised his head and tail.

"I claim victory." His voice boomed, but his tone was flat. "I claim Atiti. Does anyone else issue a challenge?"

The birds assembled in the square bowed, stretched their wings along the ground, lowered their tails, and exposed their throats. Francisco did the same, although he could not twist his head as far as the others.

"*Atiti lit orth tao de dit arknos. Okt kad men tao ressun kad edellueni Atilatiusis, avek nod Apakueni,*" everyone said. "The Atiti is strong and we are weak. Victory to him and death to Atilatius' enemies, so commands the Gods."

Sukoktheu stamped his foot.

"Indeed."

Sukoktheu glanced at Urtu: he'd stopped breathing. Without another word, the King picked up the mask-crown in his beak and strutted back into his house.

The crowd relaxed, and a group rushed to Urtu's side. Some wailed in despair, others sat silently on the ground beside his corpse. A couple went to fetch rags and did their best to wipe the blood from Urtu's feathers. By twos and threes, the crowd dispersed from King's Square, until few were left besides Urtu's mourners and the traders who were usually here.

Lord Ereter stood on the Oka'ee's end of the square, watching until the mourners carried Urtu's body away.

"Bastard." Ereter's voice was filled with barely restrained malice. "He kills his own father, and then kills his own son. I'd damn him to Restat's world, but that would be more reward than punishment. He doesn't deserve to lead."

"You could challenge him," Francisco said. Ereter coughed and turned back toward the Oka'ee ward.

"Then I'd be as dead as Laaptui Urtu."

Chapter Five

The second month of spring was So's Month, the month of lovers. Young and unmarried hens gathered in the squares of Atilatius, dolled up with freshly painted beaks and new robes, and sang of their availability to any cock who passed by. If a cock took interest, he'd introduce himself, then perform a little dance displaying the undersides of his wings and his tail feathers - a stylized form of the regular greeting ritual. If she approved, she would repeat the dance. If not, she'd sit and ignore him. If the cock was still interested, however, he'd return the next day with some sort of gift - flowers, food, perhaps a little wooden or bone-carved statuette - and try again. The back -and-forth could go on and on. Once each showed interest, they would take turns singing and dancing. This would also go on for some time, although two or three days seemed the norm, until the cock presented another gift. The hen would accept it, he'd make a show of deferring to her dominance, and the pair would be formed.

To Francisco, it seemed no different than a whore selling herself on a street corner. He was not stupid enough to say that, though.

While softer spoken than the Lord or Lady, Ereter's second wife, Useokadea, liked to micromanage. She hovered over Francisco as he worked, nitpicking at every opportunity. When he was instructed to help her prepare for Tulluedea's courtship, Francisco figured it could be an interesting diversion from Lady Itwua's endless chores. It turned out, instead, to turn his already miserable life even worse. When after a few days Ereter pulled him away to run an errand, Francisco was ready to kiss the bird's feet.

Ereter sent him to the Epotat ward, just to the south and east of the Oka'ee ward. While he was also Oka'ee-ti, Ereter was a merchant by trade and as such needed wares for when he made his biannual trips to other towns - the Epotat clan was from the Vulthaar caste, craftsmen, and made many of the valuable finished goods Oka'ee merchants traded. Ereter had been engaged in a bit of haggling by courier with Epotat Istafu over some baskets recently, a game Istafu seemed skilled at but Francisco was certain Ereter would win.

Francisco was passing through Epotat's Square on the way back when he spotted Kothidy browsing the available hens but, by the way he'd barely glance before moving on, it seemed his heart wasn't into it. He perked up when he noticed Francisco and bounded over.

"You're messenger for the Oka'ee-ti, today?" he said.

"Yes," Francisco said. "You look for a Vulthaar wife? Not an Oka'ee?"

Kothidy sighed.

"I look and look…" He let the sentence trail off. Francisco leaned close and whispered:

"You still love Tokovudea?"

"Yes." The mere mention of her seemed to sadden him. "None of these others compare."

"Then you must prove it," Francisco said. Kothidy tilted his head. "Look at me. Why do you suppose I'm here at all? I wanted to prove I was worthy of a muchacha, so I…" Maybe it wasn't such a good idea to share his murderous past with the closest thing to a friend he had here. "…I, uh, I travelled here."

"Here?"

"Yes. This place is on the other end of the world from where my people are from.   I thought perhaps demonstrating my courage would be enough to win her over. Now…"

He let himself trail off. Kothidy gestured that he understood. Francisco sighed, then continued:

"I am sure you can find some way to prove yourself a better husband for Tokovudea than Oka'ee Ithtee."

Kothidy considered that for a moment, then gestured 'Yes'.

"I understand," he said and turned away. "You have my thanks, Ransisko."

- - -

The day finally came.

To Francisco's relief, Useokadea was too concerned with Tulluedea to pester him, and Lady Itwua seemed overall disinterested in the day's affairs. Ereter met with a steady stream of callers throughout the morning; most were Oka'ee wanting some matters attended to while they still had a chance, but by midday they faded away.

In the early afternoon, birds began to gather in Oka'ee Square - Ereter, Lady Itwua and Useokadea joined them. Francisco wasn't invited, but no one seemed to object to him loitering at the edges of Ereter's property bordering the square. The square itself was shaped like an almond: fairly wide in the middle, coming to two narrow opposing ends. Along the edges, arranged in a rough circle, were five fire pits - Francisco's hands ached at the thought of digging them, bare-handed - around which food and drink were gathered. In the center of the square, Useokadea had directed him to build a mound, perhaps a foot or two tall and about five feet in diameter, with the earth dug up from the pits. Since then, it had been covered with a fur blanket, surrounded by palms, and sprinkled with red and white flower petals.

A chorus of barks interrupted the square's polite conversations, and the crowd parted at the northwest end to make way for a small army of new revelers. Their leader, the Vigsi-ti Idyllit, gestured for them to halt. He and Ereter approached each other.

"Thukomgu, Raudhua!" Idyllit said. Francisco blinked, he'd never heard anyone other than his wives call Lord Ereter by his personal name before. Ereter tilted his head back and responded with a staccato of CRAW-CRAW-CRAW's - a laugh - as well as an exaggerated bow.

"Thukomgu, you rude letch!" he replied and the two engaged in a moment or two of play fighting until their wives broke them up. "Ah, you're a sore sport, Itwua. Can't you let us have our fun?"

"No," she said. Ereter laughed again, though not as heartily, and rubbed faces with her.

"Your first wife is right," Idyllit said. "Time enough after."

"Yes, yes..."

They gestured to the Vigsi revelers to join the Oka'ee. The two mixed easily, without any hint of politicking or inter-clan rivalry. As soon as everyone settled, the square silenced while the wedding parties dispersed to the edges and left but one cock, Vigsi Elmacade, standing a dozen paces from the mound. Elmacade was splendidly dressed for the occasion: his robes were new and freshly cleaned, his necklace featured two enormous fangs amongst the feathers and claws, while his bracelets and anklets had been polished until gleaming. His tattoos looked new and his crest feathers looked particularly vibrant, perhaps they were touched up?

Francisco shook his head and sighed, he was growing far too familiar with avian fashion.

No one else was looking at Elmacade, all eyes had turned to Ereter's house. Oka'ee Tulluedea, at last, emerged: no longer did she wear the simple garb of a youngster, but now the full costume of an adult hen. She looked over the crowd and then, her manner evoking more Itwua than her mother, she assumed the dominant stance - stretched neck, raised tail. All in the square, except for Elmacade, bowed in deference and made way for her as she strutted to the mound. Tulluedea, ignoring Elmacade's presence, circled the mound once and then, approving, stepped atop and broke into song, declaring her availability. Francisco was surprised: her song was much more elegant and practiced than the almost bawdy ditties the hens in the square sang.

As she sung, it was now Elmacade's turn to circle the mound - whereas she had strutted, he pranced. When she finished singing, Elmacade stopped and the two faced each other for the first time. He bowed.

"Thuryegu, daughter of Oka'ee Ereter," he said. "I am Vigsi Elmacade Ukeu."

Elmacade then began the stylized greeting dance Francisco had seen so many times before. Unlike the ad hoc and improvised dances he'd seen in the town's squares, though, Elmacade's dance was performed with careful, practiced precision. Likewise, Tulluedea's responding dance was just as refined. To Francisco, this performance evoked the beauty and solemnity one expected of a wedding, unlike the crass solicitation and prostitution he'd previously encountered. They alternated singing and dancing two or three times each, the whole ritual going on for not quite an hour, until at last Elmacade stopped, plucked one of his own tail feathers, and presented it to Tulluedea. She accepted the gift, stuffed it into her robes, and raised her tail. Elmacade bowed deeply, his wings stretched wide and his tail feathers shuddering. Tulluedea gestured approval, stepped off the mound, and the two nuzzled each other's faces. The square erupted with barks of praise and congratulations.

As with any wedding, celebrations followed: food, drink, dancing, and music - or, at least the drums and rattles the birds of Atilatius thought of as music. The smells of roasting venison, rabbit, and not-pork ("go'sth" they called it) made Francisco's stomach growl. He sighed when he realized he probably wouldn't get any.

The day progressed and the birds grew drunker. Ereter and Idyllit cleared an area and organized games: footraces, mock fighting, and a sport they called "Pifune", or "Stick Tossing". It seemed to consist of two teams running back and forth passing a stick and one stationary team-member at an end of the playing area trying to catch it, all while the other team tried to take the stick away and pass it to their own stationary team-member. Ereter and Idyllit led opposing Oka'ee and Vigsi teams in a good-natured match, and Vigsi Elmacade seemed particularly skilled at it.

Shrieks of surprise and alarm from the southeast end of the square interrupted the match.

"What's the commotion?" Ereter said. Birds stepped aside: a cock strutted forward, his feathers splotched with dried blood, robes torn, and a carcass draped over his back.

"Kothidy!" Tokovudea pushed her way through to him. "The Gods have mercy, what's happened to you?"

"I'm fine, I'm fine," he said. By their body language, it was clear they wanted to nuzzle each other but held themselves back. For them to do so unmarried and so publicly would've been scandalous. "It's good to be home."

With a great wet plop, he tossed his prize, an enormous spotted cat, at Ereter's feet. All eyes darted to the carcass and, all at once, it seemed everyone was shouting - so quickly and loudly, Francisco couldn't hope to understand anything anyone said. Ereter and Idyllit assumed dominant stances and barked for silence, the crowd settled.

"Where did you kill this macade?" Ereter asked.

"On the east bank of Lake Asid Ovud," Kothidy said. It was a casual statement, as if the whole matter were trivial.

"Asid Ovud? That's days from here!" Ereter said. "What were you doing there?

"Proving myself a worthy husband for Tokovudea, Oka'ee-ti," Kothidy said. Ereter's head jerked back. "I searched for someone else, but no one else compares. So I…took some advice, and thought of ways I could impress you, ways I could prove myself worthy. You said I was too weak, too low ranked. Thus, I chose to hunt and kill a macade, alone. I am not weak, cousin, and I will not be low ranked for long. I will be a far better husband for your second daughter than Ithtee."

Kothidy bowed, adding a shudder to his tail feathers for emphasis.

"Oka'ee-ti, again I ask permission to marry your second daughter."

Ereter assumed the dominant stance - the Oka'ee bowed, all stepped away.

"You arrogant, thoughtless, irresponsible buffoon!" Ereter said. He did not look at Kothidy, instead strutting around him and looking as if he were addressing the crowd. "Only a fool hunts amacadieni alone. You could have been killed! Then it would have fallen to me to explain to my daughter and our kin why you were eaten by a beast. Where did you find the gall to challenge my decision, or to interrupt this celebration for Vigsi Elmacade and my first daughter?" He paused. "From my second daughter, most likely, considering how she's harried me to change my mind ever since I denied you. Where is Ithtee?"

"I am here!"

Ithtee, an older cock with a chipped beak, emerged from the revelers and bowed.

"I am withdrawing from our agreement," Ereter said. "In exchange, I will trade you one-fourth of the goods I procure from Heliokates on my next caravan. Do you agree to this new arrangement."

Ithtee did not look pleased.

"Five-twelfths would ease the pain much more easily, my leader," Ithtee said.

"CRAW! Today is a day to be generous. As you wish," Ereter said.

"You are most generous, Oka'ee-ti."

Ithtee, suddenly in a better mood, scurried back into the crowd. Ereter at last looked to Kothidy.

"Get up and clean yourself," Ereter said, his tone mock

-angry. "You must be presentable if you intend to marry my second daughter."

"Thank you!" Kothidy said. "Thank you!"

When he stood, Tokovudea pressed her side against his and the two exchanged words, too quietly for Francisco to hear from so far away. She followed him as he left the square. Ereter directed several Oka'ee to take the spotted cat away and, after that interruption, the pifune match and celebrations resumed.

At nightfall, it was Tokovudea who brought him supper - not the mush and meat he expected, but rabbit and alcohol.

"Thank you," Francisco said.

"I…I know it was you who inspired him," Tokovudea said. Francisco was surprised, those were the first words she'd ever spoken to him. "Thank you. I won't forget."

Not waiting for a response, she left and returned to the celebrations.

Per tradition, the celebration ended with the performance of a play for luck: The Newlyweds' Prayer. It began with a chorus of eight birds, half male and half female, singing a song that evoked Tokovudea's announcement song. When they finished, an older female dressed in a crude imitation of the Naeyvolis' costume, stepped into the play space and played as narrator while actors, no more than four at a time, performed as characters, singing lines and moving with purposeful motions more evocative of dance than drama. Acts, four in all, were broken up by the chorus singing imitations of the wedding duet.

The story itself was a comedy: a clan leader's daughter, Asurdea, married a rival clan member, Mimieu, against her father's wishes. The pair cooked up a scheme where he'd dress as a hen and pretend to be merely her close friend while they searched for the right time to tell the Lord. As it turned out, the Lord fell madly infatuated with "Mimtea" and decided he had to have "her" as his wife, which spurred Asurdea to assume the role of Mimtea's husband, "Asureu", and defend "his" right to "her". In the play's finale, Asureu and the Lord mock battled, the masquerade was lifted, and the lovers could at last be together in peace.

Mimieu and Asurdea were, of course, played by Elmacade and Tulluedea. Francisco was somewhat disappointed Ereter didn't play the Lord, but doubted the Oka'ee-ti had as a strong a gift for humor as the actor they chose in the end. In any case, it was at least as good as the morality plays he had seen back in Spain - Francisco couldn't think of higher praise than that.

Chapter Six

Passionate screeches woke Francisco late one night. He rolled over, hugged his deerskin blanket close, and tried to ignore the sounds of lovemaking wafting from his master's house.

Lord Ereter had grown more affectionate with his second wife as So's Month progressed, much to the chagrin of Lady Itwua. As such, the Lady became a tyrannical monster lashing verbal abuse at her servants and wasn't shy about striking Francisco when her mood soured further. He mentioned half as much to one servant when the Lady was out of earshot - the servant glowered at him (a common response to his speaking out of turn to an Auldtheu other than Kothidy).

"The first wife of Ereter cannot lay eggs anymore," she said. Francisco couldn't think of any decent response to that.

Itwua's mood sweetened after Kothidy and Tokovudea's wedding, and soon things returned to relative normalcy. The next month, rather appropriately, was called the Month of Mothers - they were only a few days into the month when Francisco learned both Useokadea and Tokovudea had laid eggs.

"Two!" Kothidy was ecstatic when Francisco next ran into him in the streets. "Tok has given me two! I'm so happy. Maybe they will be sons? I've been thinking of names, but haven't yet settled on any."

"I am happy for you," Francisco said.

"Do you have any children?" Kothidy said. Francisco frowned.

"No," he said.

"Oh." An awkward silence followed. Kothidy apologized, but Francisco told him to think nothing of it. Why should he? None of the other birds would. Kothidy stood alone in that respect, which still puzzled Francisco. Why was Kothidy so kind to him? He wanted desperately to ask, but feared the question would insult him.

Two of Useokadea's three eggs hatched fifteen days after that. Based on names alone he knew they were a girl, Keotea, and a boy, Truieu. Ereter seemed almost as giddy as Kothidy over Truieu - after now six daughters, of which only Tulluedea and Tokovudea had reached adulthood, he finally had a son. The third egg was stillborn. Ereter took it away after the others hatched and disposed of it somehow, Francisco didn't think to ask. The chicks never came outside, and Francisco rarely saw Useokadea leave the house.

Three months passed.

With no fanfare or warning, Francisco awoke one morning in late summer to discover Useokadea and the chicks outside. The chicks were chasing each other around, making little peeping and chittering sounds - not words, just meaningless babbling - while their mother sat just outside the door, enjoying the morning sun. Both chicks stood about a foot tall, one a little shorter than the other, and had feathers colored a rich earthy brown - with age, they would shift to dark gray. Even with more than a glance, Francisco couldn't tell which was which: by his untrained eye, both chicks looked like girls. The taller one stopped in its tracks when it noticed Francisco, its eyes widened and little beak hung open. Francisco sighed and went to work searching for weeds to pull.

"Hello," Francisco said, in Spanish. "Which one are you?"

The chick blinked.

"Truieu!" Useokadea said, strutting over with her miniscule tail raised. "Get away from there! Don't distract the woliothaar."

Truieu sprinted to his mother, who led him back to the house. Francisco laughed to himself and returned to weed pulling.

It wouldn't be the last encounter with Ereter's son. Truieu seemed to take an immediate liking to Francisco in the same sort of innocent friendliness a human child might have. The chick couldn't speak, he wasn't old enough yet, but his little squeaks and yips were clear enough. Most of the time Truieu would just follow Francisco around the property; sometimes, he'd try to help, but Useokadea would always interrupt. Bad enough her son was enamored with their human slave, but there was no way she'd let him start acting like one.

Lady Itwua would never object. She seemed to enjoy how much it bothered Ereter's second wife. Payback, perhaps?

Near the end of the Harvesting Month, Lord Ereter left Atilatius with his trade caravan for Lyrentasia and Maji in the west.

The plague struck a week afterward.

- - -

Illness swept across the city, striking down the powerful alongside the weak, the wealthy alongside the destitute. From his vantage point at Lord Ereter's house, Francisco watched as funeral processions passed through Oka'ee Square daily on their way to wherever it was the birds deposited their dead. Rumors spread that the Veohaulio-ti had died, and that other leaders had fallen ill.

Francisco heard more than one servant whisper, "This is Restat's doing."

Often, they would follow that with a fearful glance in Francisco's direction - he didn't quite understand why. They didn't blame him for this, did they? From the square there were cries for Dune, for the Paku-Gei, for Niwit to save Atilatius. The plague proceeded regardless.

An agonized screech woke Francisco one cold morning. At first he tried to ignore it, but then realized where it was coming from. He scrambled from his lean-to and half-ran toward the house.

"What is wrong?" he shouted, stopping just outside the doorway. "What has happened?"

A rustling within was followed by an explosion of feathers and claws.

"You! You did this!"

Francisco was knocked onto his back, his assailant battering him with her beak, and wings, and claws. He covered his face with his arms, too stunned to do anything else.

"Raudhua let you live! He let you have purpose! How could you do this to us? I thought you were different! Spawn of Restat, you monster, you fiend! My child, my child! I'll kill you! Die! Die! Die!"

As sudden as it began, the attack ended: a second force slammed into his attacker, knocking her off her feet. A loud hiss followed.

"Stop."

Francisco looked up: Lady Itwua was in the dominant stance.

"You dare take out your sorrows on Raudhua's property?" she said. Her tone was cold, passionless. "You forget yourself, Second Wife."

Useokadea appeared more than ready to redirect her fury: she was crouched, as if to pounce again.

"You defend him!" she barked.

The Lady stamped her foot and hissed again.

"Calm yourself, or you will see just how ineffective a weapon anger truly is," she said. "Go inside and tend to Raudhua's daughter. The slave is MY concern. Go. NOW!"

Useokadea shot one last hateful glare in Francisco's direction before slinking back inside. Lady Itwua turned to Francisco, her gaze upon him no less cold.

"You are injured," she said. Francisco felt battered, his arms and chest were slashed and bloody. He thanked God that Useokadea did not keep her sickle claw or beak tip sharpened, or he'd certainly have been gored to death rather than just maimed. "Return to your nest. I will send someone to tend to you later, and I will assign someone else your chores."

"Thank you," Francisco mumbled. "I don't understand…"

"Raudhua's daughter has fallen ill," Lady Itwua said.

Her dispassion masked the certainty that the child would die. "Useokadea believes that you, a child of Restat, are to blame. That is absurd. You are a beast of burden, not a demon."

She turned away and started toward the square.

"Go. I must fetch a servant of the Naeyvolis."

Francisco did has he was told. One of the Oka'ee, clearly displeased with his assignment, eventually came and dressed his wounds with salves. He tried to strike up friendly conversation, but the cock was uninterested. The birds left him alone for the rest of that day and the day after while his wounds healed somewhat. On the third day, Lady Itwua put him back to work replacing the wooden pikes that encircled the property. On that same day, Raudhua's daughter died.

The next day began the mourning. Vigsi Elmacade and Tulluedea arrived early, were greeted by Lady Itwua at the square and escorted into the house. Kothidy, Tokovudea, and their two children arrived around midday, followed shortly after by a male and female Francisco didn't know. The male and Lady Itwua nuzzled affectionately and spoke - Francisco, watching from his lean-to, couldn't make out what was said, but was surprised to see her so animated and affectionate with someone other than Lord Ereter. She escorted them inside just like the others. Beyond the usual meals at the usual times, though, Francisco was once again ignored.

On the morning of the fifth day, the three cocks emerged from the house, left, and returned after with a pallet - two long poles with an animal skin stretched between them, held aloft by robes grasped in their beaks. They reentered the house. Shortly after the entire family emerged, all - even the chicks - now wearing blank white masks which covered the tops of their beaks, their heads and faces. On the males it obscured their crest feathers, he supposed for the purpose of making each mourner look no different than any other.   One female, Useokadea he presumed, carried the child's body on her back, the corpse now entirely wrapped in in white fabric. She let it roll off her and onto the pallet, which the males and one of the females lifted with their beaks.   They then began the funeral procession: a slow, deliberate, walk, with the living crowded around the dead, all singing a mournful song interspersed with pained moans. The three chicks, all too young to at all understand what was happening, followed their mothers from close behind. Francisco watched until they all vanished beyond the square.

Lady Itwua, Useokadea, and Truieu returned alone that night, and in the days after continued wearing those white masks.   Though the mourning continued, Lady Itwua ordered him back to work.

- - -

"How can I serve you, Second Wife?"

Useokadea, paced in front of the nest hut, her white mask a little worn six days after the funeral. She rarely summoned him in the best of times, and now knowing she blamed him for her daughter's death...

His wounds still ached.

She eyed him, her face obscured by the mourning mask but her body language anything but aggressive.

"Truieu is sick."

A chill ran down Francisco's spine. He liked Truieu, the chick was the only one beside Kothidy who saw a person when looking at him.

"I am sorry," he said.

Useokadea stepped forward, half-bowing to him as

she would when showing respect to an equal. What brought this about? First she wanted to murder him, now this?

"Please...do something..." she said. "I know you are fond of him. I know you would not want him to die. Please, if you can intercede on his behalf...convince Restat to spare him..."

Francisco frowned.

"My people call him el diablo," he said. "And we are just as fearful and helpless before him as you. If I could do anything, I promise you I would do it."

"You can do nothing?"

"I am sorry," Francisco said. She studied him for a long silent moment before dismissing him. He returned to his lean-to and, little else to do, he wrapped himself in his blanket and prayed. The chick was as mild and innocent as any human boy, and if these birds were God's creatures as men were, then Truieu deserved the Lord's protection as well. Francisco rummaged through the few things he had until he found a length of twine, left over from the last time he'd repaired a fishing net. Finding two small sticks, he bound them together into an imitation crucifix. With a bit more twine he fashioned it into a necklace. It was crude, but it was something. When one of the Lady's servants delivered his nightly meal he handed the bird the cross and told him to give it Useokadea.

"What is it?" the bird said.

"Tell her it will protect Ereter's son from Restat."

The bird gestured in the affirmative and left.

Over the next seven days Francisco made every effort to eavesdrop on the servants' chatter in the hopes of learning anything, but heard little more than gossip. Lady Itwua never engaged in such discussions and Useokadea never left her son's side, leaving him at a complete loss.

Admirable, but frustrating! Was no one else concerned, or even just curious, about the child? Every morning and night he'd query, and either got no response or plain ignorance. It didn't help that many of the servants still felt as Useokadea had and saw Francisco as the source of the city's troubles. To think, over a year ago he was debating whether or not these birds were hell spawn, and all the while they had simply assumed he was a servant of Satan! It made Francisco even more curious about Kothidy than he already was.

Francisco got his answer on the eighth day.

"Truieu!"

The chick, somewhat emaciated and missing a good deal of feathers, trotted up to Francisco in good spirits and seeming well despite his appearance.

"You're feeling better?" Francisco said, in Spanish. The chick yipped excitedly and ran a couple circles around Francisco, before stopping himself and, to Francisco's surprise, gesturing in the affirmative. "I'm glad. Very glad."

Francisco then noticed that along with his little white mourning mask, Truieu wore nothing else...except for the makeshift crucifix dangling from his neck. He glanced toward the house and spotted Useokadea sunning outside, watching, but making no move to intervene. Truieu didn't notice: he was too busy starting the hunt for weeds and worms.

Francisco laughed.

"Yes," he said, again in Spanish. "Back to work, little one!"

Chapter Seven

Lord Ereter returned at the end of the month.

Francisco was not present to see how he reacted to the news of the plague or his daughter's death, but the next time he saw the bird he was wearing a mourning mask. More than once Francisco noticed Ereter watching him from afar, but since his owner made no moves toward him he pretended not to notice.

The last week of Dune's Month was a weeklong holiday called 'Resth', a word he took to be an antiquated form of the birds' word for 'farewell'. The holiday was already solemn in nature, but in the aftermath of the plague it took on an extra dose of melancholy. The King still took the opportunity to reward birds who had gained his favor in recent months, and contests were still held. The city has a whole, however, did not seem to have its collective heart in it.

Francisco had finished his meal and was warming himself beside the small fire the birds tolerated him lighting each night when Ereter suddenly emerged from the shadows. Francisco yelped.

"Ah! I am sorry, you startled me."

Lord Ereter stood over Francisco studying him, not in the dominant stance but his power over the young man still felt. Francisco gulped.

"Can I serve you, Master?"

"My wife tells me you saved my son," Ereter said.

"All I did was give him the crucifix and pray that my God would protect him," Francisco said.

"Crucifix?" Ereter's accent maimed the unfamiliar word. "That was the icon you gave my son?"

"Yes."

"And this…" He paused. "This cross thing is the symbol of your God?"

"Yes."

"Then I am in debt to you and your God for saving my son's life," Ereter said. "My second wife believes he would have died that night had you not intervened. Instead, he lives. You have my gratitude."

Ereter half-bowed. Francisco, from where he sat, returned the gesture.

"I will not forget this," Ereter said. "I know you desire freedom, but trust my words when I say to free you would mean your certain death at the claws of either Sukoktheu himself or a Laaptui warrior. You will remain here, a slave in name but otherwise free to do as you will amongst the Oka'ee."

Francisco bowed again.

"Thank you, Master."

Lord Ereter turned to leave.

"Do you have a name?" he said.

"Francisco. Francisco del Puerto."

Ereter paused, perhaps committing the name to memory, then returned to the night from whence he came.

Appendix

Eliohaar (derived from the Atilatian phrase "lio thaar", meaning "winged people"; taxonomically Cariama *Sapiens*, derived from the Tupi word "çariama", meaning "crested", and the Latin "sapiens", meaning "wise") are, besides humans, the only other sapient species on Earth. Along with the Seriema, they are the only surviving Cariamiformes, an order of primarily flightless birds which also included the Phorusrhacids (also known as the "terror birds"). Recent theories dispute the traditional view, however, and instead posit that the eliohaar actually belong to the family Dromaeosauridae.

The earliest ancestors evolved around 3 million years ago in South America. It is believed that the social and aggressive behavior developed as an adaptation against mammalian predators invading from North America. Modern eliohaar appeared in Uruguay around 350,000 years ago and quickly spread over South America as far north as Venezuela and Colombia, with some recent archaeological evidence suggesting tribes as far north as the southern United States. The species proved highly adaptable, and was able to survive the Ice Age without any appreciable dwindling in the population.

The appearance of humans 15,000 to 25,000 years ago resulted in a crisis as the two species competed for dominance. Being technologically and cognitively equivalent, as well as both being apt in the art of war, the result was a stalemate that split the Americas into a human North and eliohaaran South. This balance was disrupted by the introduction of archery by Arctic traders 2,500 years ago, which native human Americans used to great effect in hunting and warfare. By 500 A.D., humans had come to dominate everything north of the Paraná River and along the Andes mountains.

II

Eliohaaran naming conventions differ amongst the species' four major cultural groups: the Yvathaareni, the Corarnotics, the Smoezoekoe, and the Southerners.

Yvathaareni names

Amongst the Yvathaareni tribes and city-states, names are generally constructed in the form of:

[Family Name] [Given Name] [Secondary Name].

Family names are often descriptive, either of the family's profession (ex. "Ythotheo", Majinese for "Warrior") or a shared physical attribute (ex. "Laaptui", Atilatian for "Black-Breasted").

Given names are almost universally constructed in the form of an adjective-noun compound word (ex. "Iedue", Tolsaari for "Blue Feather") and are used primarily in formal situations, or when casually addressing a non-relative or an acquaintance. Given names have a special cultural significance, being imparted only to males in a ritualistic ceremony upon reaching sexual maturity, usually around eight years old. It is extremely rare for a female to have a Given Name.

Secondary names are imparted upon males and females at birth, generally a simple noun followed by a suffix. The suffix would depend upon the linguistic norms of the given tribe. For example, amongst the Heliokatics the convention was "-hua" for eldest male siblings, and "-wua" for females or younger male siblings; for the Atilatians, however, convention held that male secondary names ended in "-eu" while female names ended in "-tea" or "-dea". Secondary names are used by family members or close friends as a sign of intimacy, and are considered rude to use in a more public setting. Since females only have secondary names, they are publicly addressed as "[Ranked] Wife of [Husband]", "Daughter of [Father]", "Mother of [Son]" or "Sister of [Brother]". The exception to the rule being the case of a female imparted with a Given Name.

III

Religious Beliefs

Pakuism, also known as **Uaaryan religion** or **Du**, is a religion practiced by the Yvathaareni eliohaar of Argentina and Uruguay in South America. It was founded in the city of Uaarya sometime before the 1st Century AD.

A polytheistic religion, adherents worship a pantheon of gods and goddesses that are believed to have dominance over realms of nature and the universe. Chief amongst these gods, or "Paku", are the four Paku-ki or "third gods": Duahib (goddess of agriculture, dance, and pleasure), Heyforth (god of war and duels), So (goddess of love and hatchlings), and Dune (god of wisdom, knowledge, and speech). Uaaryans also believe in the existence of an afterlife ruled by two additional gods, Restat and Niwit, who are associated with death and life.

Pakuist beliefs were the official religion in Atilatius, Heliokates, and Zanados when Spanish conquistadors arrived in the region in the early 16th Century. In the centuries since then, the number of adherents has dwindled to only a fraction of the eliohaaran population.

Creation Myth

Pakuists believe the universe began as chaos, and from that chaos emerged an egg which hatched the first beings: Danoolfeo (the Sun) and Naedisfeo (the Moon). These two Paku came together and hatched a child, Megikua, the God of Creation. Megikua, seeing the chaos around them, decided to bring order to the world by dismembering himself. His blood became Reos (the Sea), his breath became Raud (the Sky), his flesh became Ib (the Land), and his feathers became the creatures, both plant and animal, of the world. Reos, Raud, and Ib ruled over the world in peace for many eons, until one day Raud grew jealous of his siblings and warred with them for control of the world.

The Gods warred for 1,024 years, until at last Niwit (Life), the son of Raud, appeared and plead with the Gods for peace. Niwit was respected by everyone in the world as a wise, Just, and peaceful deity, and his pleas convinced the Gods to stop fighting. So happy and grateful for what he did, Niwit was crowned Veoti (King) of the world. Veoti Niwit commanded the eliohaar to build him the first city, which when complete he named Qatdus, or "God's City". There he ruled and all was well for another 1,024 years.

Eventually, the power granted Veoti Niwit corrupted him. He grew evil and corrupt, oppressing all of the world. This darkness went on for generations, until at last the eliohaar grew tired of his rule and, in a great coup, they rose up against him. After a tremendous battle, they overthrew the evil God-King and banished him from Megikua's world. Trapped outside, the good and evil within Niwit fought for control until at last the God tore himself in half. The good half adopted the name Niwit, while the evil half named himself Restat (death). The two Gods created their own worlds, and populated them with the souls cast out of Megikua's world.

Seeing the world needed a ruler, the children of Ib (Duahib and Heyforth) and the children of Reos (So and Dune), claimed joint leadership over the world. They decided an eliohaar should rule over Qatdus, and challenged the mortals to present the strongest amongst them. The eliohaar established an order and the strongest became Veoti of Qatdus.

Distinguishing Characteristics

Pakuist religious practices are geared toward both strength and acting honorably, with the belief that only the strong and honorable could defeat the warriors of Restat awaiting souls in the afterlife and be seen as worthy of living in Niwit's world. High virtues are considered to be wisdom and charity, and amongst most practitioners Dune is the most revered God. Pride, irresponsibility, thoughtlessness, and wrath are associated with Restat and, thus, discouraged.

Practitioners worship together in large groups, mostly

on holidays, in generally joyous although occasionally solemn celebrations. Holidays always involve large feasts, with the food ceremonially gifted to the associated God or Gods and then eaten throughout the day. Prayer involves a leader, either a shaman-like figure called the "Naeyvolis" or an eliohaar assuming the role of a mythological figure, reciting religious verse while the others respond. Yvathaareni drama is an extension of this practice, and as a result bears similarity to Ancient Greek drama.

IV

Uaaryan drama, also known as **Pakunodun** (Heliokatic for "Prayer"), is a performance art that emerged amongst the Yvathaareni eliohaar of South America during the 1st Millenium AD. It is the most well-known form of Eliohaaran literature, and is believed to have emerged out of the Pakuist religious practice of group prayer. While common to all Yvathaareni and many Eastern Eliohaar, the art was most refined and prominent in the city-state of Heliokates.

Origins

It is unknown when, exactly, the Yvathareeni eliohaar began performing drama, although historians often suggest the 1st Century AD. In Eliohaaran Myths and Folklore, Dr. Janice Harker theorized the division did not emerge until after the fall of the Uaaryan Empire in the 8th

Century AD. Drama is a form of religious expression in Pakuism, and traditionally performances coincide with religious holidays. By the 16th Century, secular topics and storylines had begun to emerge within the form. The most famous Yvathaareni plays, the Balan Cycle, recount the history of the Lyrentasian Empire, heavily embellished and told in a religious context.

Pakuism does not differentiate between group prayer or drama, both considered different forms of "pakunodun". Traditional group prayer features a leader, called the Naeyvolis, engaging in a mock dialogue with worshipers, often in the form song or verse. Certain prayers require the Naeyvolis, or a stand-in, to take on the role of a mythological figure. This practice, at some undetermined time, grew to include multiple actors, storylines, and performances that eventually distinguished Uaaryan drama as an artform.

Uaaryan drama was passed down for at least one thousand years as part of the Yvathaareni oral tradition before being first recorded by Jesuit missionaries in the mid-to-late 16th Century.

Genres

Uaaryan drama has three genres: Tragedy, Comedy, and Epic.

Tragedies are differentiated from the other two genres in that the protagonist always dies at the end of the play. Plots deal with the death of a Chief or King, a disaster of some sort, or a defeat in battle. The Heliokatic word for tragedy, "kyencao", translates literally as "sad song". Comedies are more light-hearted than tragedies or epics, dealing with humorous or romantic topics. Common plots include humorous misunderstandings, the pairing of an King or Chief male with a lower ranked female, or the events surrounding a birth. The Heliokatic word for comedy, "hadacao", translated literally is "happy song". Epics cover serious subject matters, like tragedies, but end on a happy note. Common subjects include the story of a victorious battle or of a King or Chief's journey away from the tribe. The Heliokatic word for this genre, "fotharaht", translates into English as "fighting song".

All three genres of Uaaryan drama – Tragedy, Comedy, and Heroic – follow the same basic structure, despite their varying topics and moods. Like Greek drama, there is a chorus, a role usually fulfilled by the audience, and actors – but, similar to Renaissance drama, violent actions are performed on stage and not implied. Unlike South Eliohaaran drama, the structure is rather rigid and each play is expected follow a specific format:

Prologue Song
Exposition, or Inciting Incident
First Reprise
Development
Second Reprise
The Twist
Final Reprise
Climax and Resolution
Denouement Song

Each genre has its own variations and conventions, but ultimately each follows the same basic structure.

V

Unlike humans, eliohaaran body types do not vary substantially from individual to individual. Members of the species use other cues, such as revealing the unique pattern of feathers under their wings or smell, to tell each other apart. Humans, not having evolved with the sensitivity toward non-visual cues, often report difficulty in telling one individual eliohaar from another unless they have had substantial and prolonged enough contact with a given individual. Although body size is largely determined by genes, it is also significantly influenced by environmental factors such as diet and exercise. The average height of an adult eliohaar is 1.07 meters (3 feet 5 inches) to 1.4 meter (4 feet 5 inches) tall, although this varies significantly from place to place and depending on ethnic origin.

Females will lay two to three 3-inch long eggs, which hatch after about 30 to 45 days. Eliohaaran chicks are on average about 2.75 in. (7 cm.) in length, and grow quickly during the first few months:

4 Weeks: 6.35 in. (16.1 cm.)
8 Weeks: 10 in. (25.4 cm.)
12 Weeks: 1 ft. 2 in. (35.6 cm.)

After twelve weeks, growth rapidly subsides At 7 months, what is colloquially considered "one eliohaaran year" in the same sense as "dog years" or "cat years", chicks average 1 ft. 5 in. (43.2 cm.) in height. By one full year, chicks stand at about 2 ft. (61 cm.). Eliohaar generally stay around that height throughout childhood, growing to about 2 ft. 6 in. (76.2 cm.) by the time they reach sexual maturity at 8 years. They go through a growth spurt between the ages 9 and 11 after which they achieve their adult height, usually somewhere between 3 ft. 5 in. (1.07 m.) and 4 ft. 5 in. (1.4 m.)

About the Author

A writer for as far back as he could remember, Paul V. Cwiakala was raised on a steady diet of Science Fiction, Fantasy, and Adventure movies ranging from novels by Harry Turtledove and H. G. Wells to movies written by Shinichi Sekizawa and Lawrence Kasdan. Having written short stories throughout his youth, Paul wrote his first novel while pursuing undergraduate studies at William Paterson University, where he earned a Bachelor's Degree in Communications in 2009.

Paul published his first novel, *Fallen Saints*, through Silk Baron Independent Press in 2014. A *Slave of the Bird Men* was previously published in Innovate E-Magazine issues #8, #9, and #10. This is the first time it has been collected and published as a standalone work.

Also Available From
Silk Baron Independent Press

FALLEN SAINTS

AN ANCIENT RELIC. POWERFUL FANATICS.
A WOMAN AND HER GUN.

Two thousand years ago, the Power of God and the ability to perform powerful magic were revealed to the world. Protected by the Church, only the powerful magic-wielding "Miracle Workers" today know these divine secrets.

Now, in an American Old West where gunslingers and magic are facts of everyday life, Angie Grissom and her Cajun partner, Andrew Carnation, hunt down criminals for cash with little more than their wits and brawn. But when the hunt for a simple thief puts her in the middle of a religious blood feud between two factions of fanatical Miracle Workers and a battle over an ancient book with ties to the very origin of their powers, will Angie's quick draw be enough?

Action and adventure await in a Wild West that never was!